D1099816

This Book Belongs to:

. . . . . .

For Tremayne and Piers

First published in Great Britain in 1982 by
Andersen Press Ltd., 20 Vauxhall Bridge Road, London SW1V 2SA.
This paperback edition first published in 2008 by Andersen Press Ltd.
Published in Australia by Random House Australia Pty.,
Level 3, 100 Pacific Highway, North Sydney, NSW 2060.
Text copyright © Hiawyn Oram, 1982.
Illustration copyright © Satoshi Kitamura, 1982.
The rights of Hiawyn Oram and Satoshi Kitamura to be identified as the author and illustrator of this work have been asserted by them in accordance with the Copyright, Designs and Patents Act, 1988. All rights reserved.
Colour separated in Switzerland by Photolitho AG, Zürich.
Printed and bound in Malaysia by Tien Wah Press.

10 9 8 7 6

British Library Cataloguing in Publication Data available.

ISBN 978 1 84270 774 6

# Angry Arthur

Hiawyn Oram  Satoshi Kitamura

ANDERSEN PRESS

Once there was a boy called Arthur.
He wanted to stay up and watch
the western on T.V.

10588,401/ JIF

WESTMEATH COUNTY LIBRARY

"No," said his mother,
"it's too late. Go to bed."
"I'll get angry," said Arthur.
"Get angry,"
said his mother.

So he did. Very, very angry.
He got so angry that his anger became a stormcloud
exploding thunder and lightning and hailstones.

"That's enough,"
said his mother.
But it wasn't.

Arthur's anger became a hurricane hurling rooftops and chimneys and church spires.

164-US

"That's enough,"
said his father.
But it wasn't.

Arthur's anger became a typhoon
tipping whole towns
into the seas.

TYPhoonTea
14
PUTNEY

"That's enough," said his grandfather.
But it wasn't.

Arthur's anger became an earth tremor cracking the surface of the earth like a giant cracking eggs.
"That's enough," said his grandmother.
But it wasn't.

Arthur's anger became a universequake

WESTMEATH COUNTY LIBRARY

and the earth and the moon

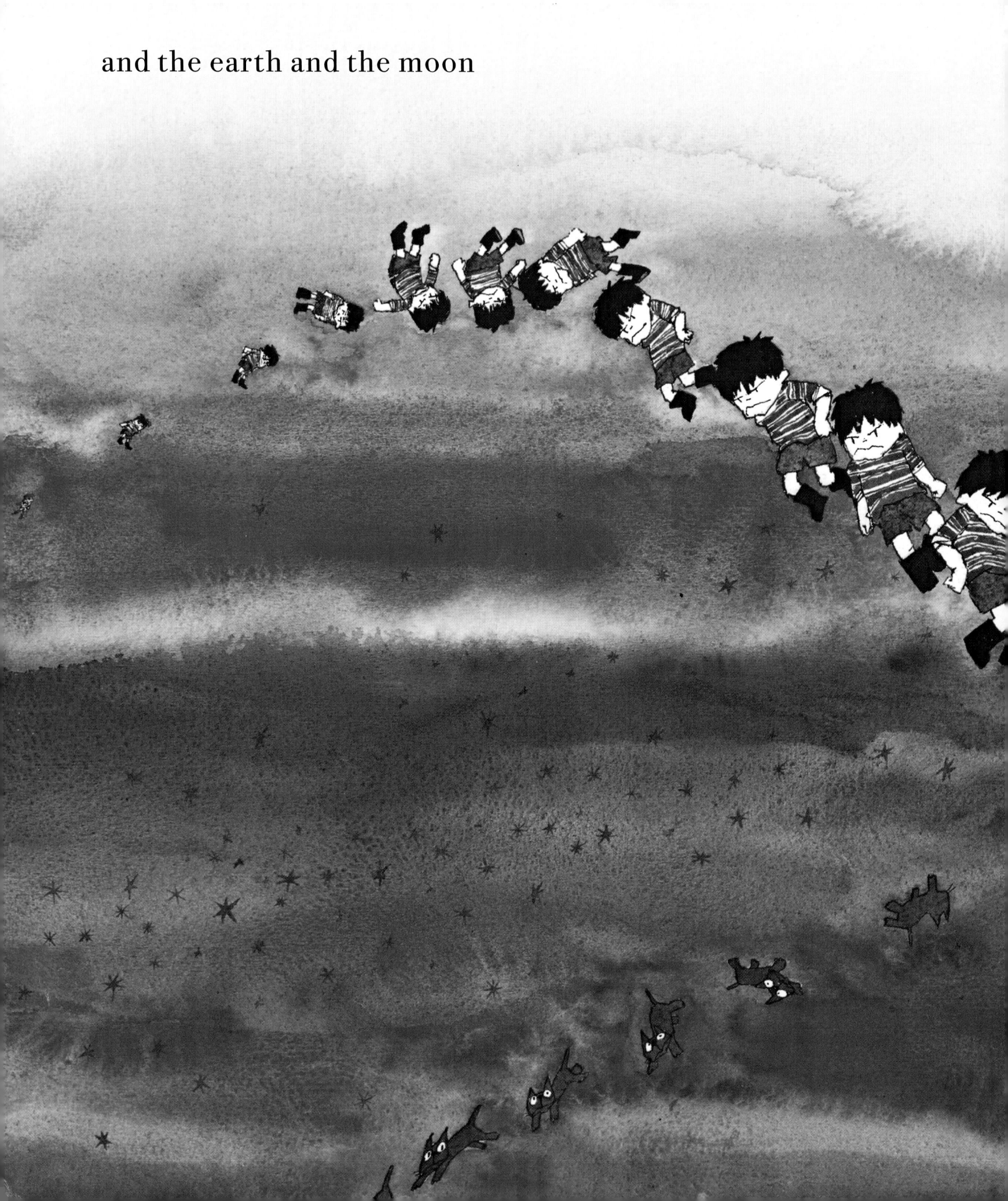

and the stars and the planets,

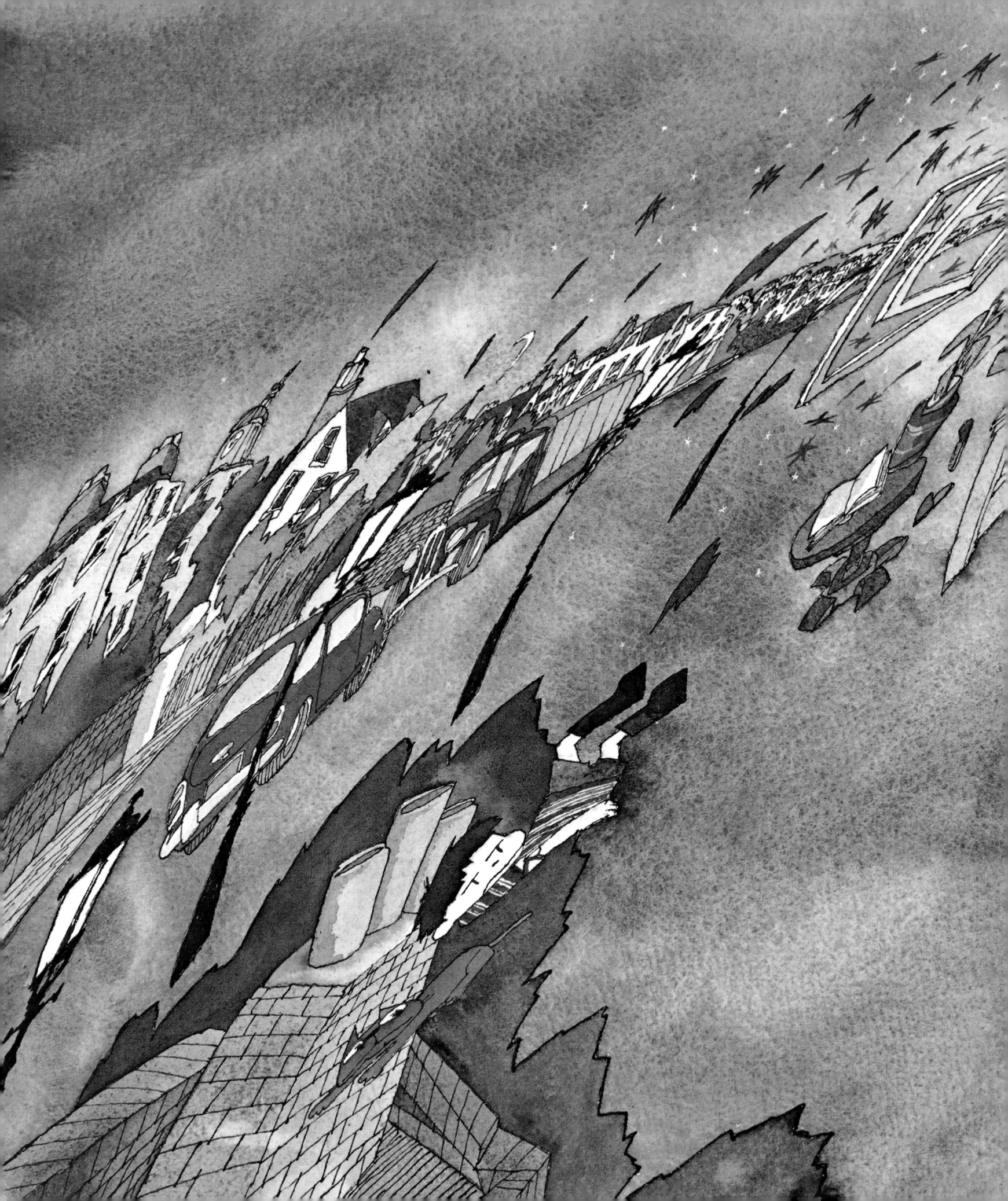

Arthur's country and Arthur's town, his street,
his house, his garden and his bedroom

were nothing more
than bits in space.

Arthur sat on a piece of Mars and thought.
He thought and thought.

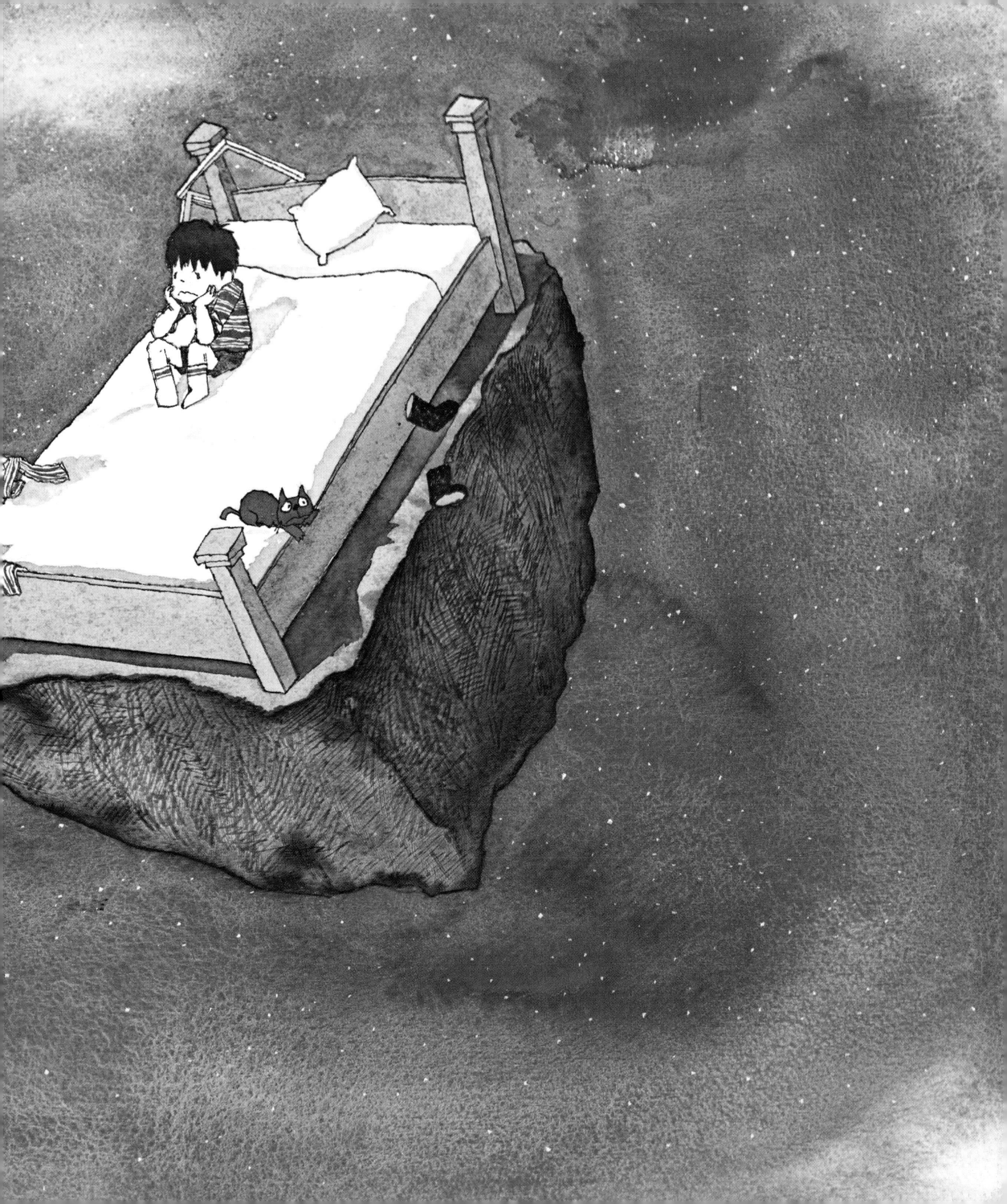

"Why was I so angry?" he thought.
He never did remember.
Can you?

WESTMEATH COUNTY LIBRARY
3 0019 00398504 5

# Other titles by

# Satoshi Kitamura

A Boy Wants a Dinosaur (text by Hiawyn Oram)

Comic Adventures of Boots

From Acorn to Zoo: and Everything in Between

Igor, The Bird Who Couldn't Sing

In the Attic (text by Hiawyn Oram)

Me and My Cat?

Ned and the Joybaloo (text by Hiawyn Oram)

Once Upon an Ordinary School Day (text by Colin McNaughton)

Pablo the Artist

Sheep in Wolves' Clothing

UFO Diary

What's Inside?

What's Wrong With My Hair?

When Sheep Cannot Sleep